MW01690734

SWELL

Edited by Peter S. Conrad
With an Introduction by
Steven Weissman

Infospect Press

Published by Infospect Press, 17681 Foster Road, Los Gatos, California, 95030.

Conrad, Peter S, 1968-
Swell
p. cm.
ISBN 0-9670268-1-4
1. Cartoons and comics. 2. Comic books, strips, etc.

741.5973 Swell

ISBN 0-9670268-1-4 (pbk.)

5 4 3 2 1

This book is dedicated to the dimensions of width and height, without which there would be no comics at all.

Special thanks to:
Shannon, for the words of encouragement and discouragement;
Arcadia, for putting up with late-night work on comics and anthologies;
Alastair, for the infrastructure;
Jill, for hanging in there;
Mike, for hunting blurbs;
Kevin, for promotion;
Greg, for the two-five;
Eric, for the tenacity;
Dirk, for the kind words;
Scott, for the exclamation point;
Filip and Robert at Diamond;
and all the individual contributors to *Swell*.

Order more copies of Swell using this convenient form!

Name ______________________________

Address ______________________________

____

City ____________ **State** ______ **Zip** ______

Please send me ____ **copies of Swell.**

Mail this form and payment to:

Peter S. Conrad
P. O. Box 64522
Sunnyvale, CA 94088

Swell is $7.95 postage paid. California residents add 8.25% sales tax. Please allow 4-6 weeks delivery time. If you order more than ten copies, there is a 60% discount.

Contents

Contents

Contents

Contents

Introduction

Introductions are tricky and, very often, stupid. This one is neither. It is by Steven Weissman of San Francisco, California.

THINGS GET A LITTLE EASIER...
ONCE YOU UNDERSTAND
I'LL BE EXPECTING YOU TO GET A HAIRCUT BY FRIDAY!
FORGET IT, DAD! THAT WON'T CHANGE ANYTHING!
FORGET NOTHING! YOU'LL DO AS I SAY AS LONG AS YOU'RE LIVING IN MY HOUSE!
HE KNOW'S I'M NOT FEELING WELL, AND YET HE DOESN'T TAKE ONE SECOND TO HELP HIS MOTHER! HIS ONLY CONCERN IS FOR HIMSELF!
C'MON, MOM! WHAT DO YOU WANT FROM ME?
DON'T ARGUE WITH YOUR MOTHER! JUST SHUT UP AND LISTEN!!
BUT, MOM! ALL MY FRIENDS WILL BE THERE!
I SAID NO! YOU CAN'T GO!
BUT WHY?
I DON'T WANT YOU IN THAT NEIGHBORHOOD!
WHY? WHAT'S WRONG WITH THE NEIGHBORHOOD?
ARE YOU SURE NO ONE KEPT YOU COMPANY WHILE YOU WERE BABYSITTING?
I DON'T LIKE THE KIND OF PEOPLE LIVING THERE!
WHAT'S WRONG WITH THEM?
NEVER MIND, SOME DAY YOU'LL THANK ME!
WHAT'S THAT SUPPOSED TO MEAN?
JUST CURIOUS.
ADMIT IT, MOM! YOU DON'T TRUST ME!
THINGS GET A LITTLE EASIER, ONCE YOU UNDERSTAND...

WHERE ARE YOU GOING NOW?
MY FRIEND'S HOUSE.
DON'T YOU HAVE THINGS TO DO IN THE HOUSE? DON'T YOU HAVE ANY HOMEWORK? WHY DON'T YOU SIT DOWN AND READ A BOOK?!
OH, MA.
MA, I'LL BE HOME AT ELEVEN.
YOU'D BETTER BE HOME AT TEN OR DON'T BOTHER TO COME HOME AT ALL!
DON'T "OH, MA" ME! YOU'RE WASTING YOUR LIFE AWAY WITH FOOLISH THINGS!
WHAT ARE YOU TALKING ABOUT? HOW ABOUT YOUR BRIDGE CLUB AND YOUR LADIES' GROUPS AND YOUR TEA PARTIES AND DAYTIME PROGRAMS? WHAT ABOUT ALL THAT?
THAT'S DIFFERENT.
HEY, DAD, DID YOU SEE MY NEW GUITAR? I JOINED A GROUP!
SON, THERE'S A LITTLE BIT MORE TO LIFE THAN JOINING A GROUP!
WHEN I WAS YOUR AGE, I WAS WORKING 12 HOURS A DAY, 6 DAYS A WEEK, I ONLY GOT PAID FOR THE FOOD AND RENT!
I DON'T GET IT! WHAT'S THAT GOT TO DO WITH ME?
IF YOU CAN'T FIGURE IT OUT FOR YOURSELF, YOU'RE STUPID!!
YEAH, DAD? WHAT IS THERE TO LIFE?
MR. COOK?
YES?
YOU HAVE A SON NAMED ROBERT? ROBERT COOK, AGE 17?
YES.
I'M SORRY, MR. COOK. YOU'D BETTER COME DOWN TO THE STATION HOUSE WITH ME... YOUR SON IS DEAD.
DEAD? HOW?!
HE DIED OF AN OVERDOSE.
OH MY GOD!!
THINGS GET A LITTLE EASIER, ONCE YOU UNDERSTAND...
"ONCE YOU UNDERSTAND" (L. STALLMAN/B. SUSSER) ©1972 SONGS FOR EVERYBODY (BMI)
ART ©2001 SAM HENDERSON
THANKS TO IRWIN CHUSID

The Forbidden Desire

By Dearand. 1998.

The Rabbi Elias Kazan was worried about his life.
In the afternoon while he was praying in the synagogue he thought about his only desire on the earth.

His rabbi friends laughed at him
I'M SO HAPPY...
But he went on seeking.
THE EFT RABBI
Fifty years later, he got his bodily change.
Now nobody would intimate with him again or touch his holy surname.
THE END!
2

NEIL JAM
YOU'RE BEING AWFULLY QUIET. WHAT'S ON YOUR MIND?

I DON'T BELIEVE IT.
WHAT IS IT?
THERE SHE IS! RIGHT OVER THERE!
WHAT SHOULD I DO TO GET HER ATTENTION?
I DON'T KNOW... THROW SOMETHING AT HER.
BONK

THERE'S SO MUCH I'D LIKE TO SAY TO YOU.
I WANT TO TELL YOU ABOUT MY DREAMS AND FEARS.
I WANT TO TELL YOU ABOUT MY FEELINGS.
I FEEL THAT YOU UNDERSTAND ME.
ARE YOU TALKING TO ME?
FITZ'02

Happy end

dead
end

"harmony" ©2001 Jesse Reklaw

THERE WERE, OF COURSE, QUESTIONS TO BE ANSWERED.
WORK, THE NEXT DAY?
FOOD? NO, HE WASN'T HUNGRY.
maybe some more to drink?
A MAN ON A BEACH?
MAN
BEACH
SMOKING?
ALONE?
WHERE IS HE GOING?
DID HE LOVE HIS MOTHER?
IS THAT REALLY HIS PIPE?

THERE WAS AN URGE TO SHUT THE OTHER WINDOW. JUST ONE SEEMED IMBALANCED, AND BESIDES, IT WAS GETTING COLD.
HE MUMBLED SOME EXCUSE ABOUT ADAPTING TO ONE'S ENVIRONMENT.
BUT ULTIMATELY HE WAS TOO DRUNK AND UNINSPIRED TO CLOSE IT.
ANOTHER MAN, AN ISLAND, LUSH BUT DESERTED.
IT COULD BE THE SAME MAN FROM THE BEACH. PERHAPS HE SWAM ACROSS.
PERHAPS NOT.
BETTER THAT THEY'RE DIFFERENT, IDENTICAL TWINS IN FACT.
SEPARATED BY SHIP-WRECK.
ONE CHILD LOST AT SEA WASHES ASHORE AND LIVES IN SOLITUDE.

THE OTHER INHERITS HIS FATHER'S GARMENT FACTORY, BUT LIVES HIS LIFE MISUNDERSTOOD, ANGRY, DESPERATE FOR A HUMAN CONNECTION.
IN THESE 34 YEARS, THE TWINS' EYES HAD NOT MET UNTIL THAT MOMENT ON OPPOSING BEACHES.
THOUGH 3000 MILES ACROSS AN INDIFFERENT OCEAN, THE LIGHT BOUNCED FROM ONE PAIR OF RETINAS TO THE OTHER IN JUST A SIXTIETH OF A SECOND.
NEITHER MAN SAW ANYTHING OF COURSE. BUT IT REMAINS AN INCREDIBLE COINCIDENCE.
you're the twin who will be lost at sea.
no, you are.
PRESENTLY HE FELL ASLEEP AND AWOKE WITH AN ACUTE NECK PAIN THAT LINGERED FOR OVER A WEEK.

LIKE MOST PEOPLE, HE HAD A GENERAL DISTASTE FOR SOCIETY AND ITS MECHANISMS.
OUT OF PLACE.
IT OFTEN PROVOKED HIM TO TAKE SOLITARY VACATIONS THAT LASTED HOURS, OR EVEN DAYS.
HAHA HA HA
HA
A HIKE IN THE FOOTHILLS, A LONG WALK BESIDE THE TRAIN TRACKS.
HAAAA
sob
BUT NOT BEING TRAPPED ON A DESERT ISLAND, HE ALWAYS FOUND AN EXCUSE TO RETURN.
this stop- broadwa
ONCE SETTLED BACK IN, THE REASONS TO ESCAPE FESTERED AND MULTIPLIED.
Request for Leave
From
To
THIS TIME HE RESOLVED TO GO TO THE BEACH.
what's the occasion?
family reunion.
UNFORTUNATELY, SOLITARY THOUGHT COULD BE DECEIVING.
FALSE SOLUTIONS CRYSTALLIZED AND SEEMED EASY TO WASH AWAY.
WHILE THE REAL PROBLEM LURKED BENEATH THE SURFACE OF THE INQUIRY.

THE TRICK WAS TO ATTACK ONE'S CON-VICTIONS, TRY TO SEE THINGS FROM MULTIPLE ANGLES.
BUT THEN IT WAS EASY TO REACH A STALEMATE, OR LOSE SIGHT OF THE QUESTION ALTOGETHER.
IN THE END, HE RELIED ON GUT FEELING AND COMFORTED HIMSELF WITH THE BELIEF THAT LOGIC HAD FAILED TO PROVE ONE THING OR ANOTHER.
IT WASN'T THE MOST ELEGANT SOLUTION.
BUT THEN AGAIN...
IT WASN'T A VERY INTERESTING PROBLEM TO BEGIN WITH.
i quit.

end.

PIXELVISION
AT SIX A.M. I EAT LEFTOVER BEANS AND RICE, WATCHING T.V. ...
A heeh-heh -heh!
That's right, and here's another great summer gift!
GRILLIN' IT!
?

I THINK:
I MEAN, WE DON'T EVEN KNOW HOW A RADIO WAVE REALLY WORKS! OR TV!
"IT JUST DOES."
TAKA-
TAKA-
TAKA-
TAKA-
TAKA-
I IMAGINE MY BRAIN SPLITTING LIKE AN ATOM FROM A QUARTER CENTURY OF RADIO WAVES, GAMMA RAYS, AND WHO KNOWS WHAT ELSE, SHOOTING THROUGH MY SKULL.

MY BONES MELT AND DROOP FROM THE CONSTANT BOMBARDMENT, AS PIXEL BY PIXEL A SITUATION COMEDY FROM 1974 PASSES THROUGH MY BODY AND ZOOMS DOWN THE STREET.
YUM!
30% OF WHAT'S IN MY STOMACH LOOKS LIKE SUZANNE SOMMERS.

I FEEL SICK
CLACK
4213
THE FADING STARS SEEM BRIGHTER THAN THEY SHOULD
ZACK SOTO 2001

ESCAPE!
©2000 KPC
FASTER! FASTER!! WE GOTTA GET OUT! GOTTA ESCAPE! HURRY DOWN THIS LONG DARK CORRIDOR! GO! GO! GOING!
THE LIGHT AT THE END SHINES UPON OUR BROWS! IT IS OUR SALVATION! GOTTA GET TO IT! IT IS OUT! OUT OF THIS DARK TUNNEL! FAST! FASTER!
BEHIND US IS THE BLAST! THE FIERY BOOM DOOM, DOOMING US! PROPELLING US ONWARD DOWN THE TUNNEL! ESCAPE! ESCAPE!
BUT THERE IS A MEMBRANE- SOFT, GIVING! WE TEAR RIGHT THROUGH IT-THAT SPONGY, MOIST MEMBRANE! OUT INTO THE LIGHT!
STRIKING HOME! WE ESCAPE TO THE OUTSIDE-SO OPEN, SO FREE! NEVER MIND THE TUNNEL, NEVER MIND THE SOFT RUBBERY MEMBRANE STILL STICKING TO US!
LANDING FINALLY-THE SURFACE GIVES A LITTLE FROM OUR FLIGHT! BUT IT IS REST, ESCAPE! IT IS OVER!
AWAY AND HERE, NEAR AND AWAY BUT AT LAST FREE! WE ESCAPED...
WE MADE IT!!!
DEDICATED TO DEADBONE.

OBSOLESCENCE
©KPC'01
...AND AS STOCKS CONTINUE TO PLUMMET TODAY, NEBULA MICRO-CONDUCTORS LAID OFF ANOTHER 5000 EMPLOYEES. A KEY SPOKES PERSON FOR THE COMPANY SAID: "WE JUST NEEDED THE SPACE". AND NOW HERE'S LINDA FLAGSTAFF WITH OUR "EYE ON SCIENCE"... LINDA...
THANKS BRETT...
WELL, MANY OF YOU MAY REMEMBER DR. JOSEPH LEIGHTON'S CAMPAIGN TO BAN PAIN RELIEVERS AUGUST LAST YEAR...
AND MANY OF YOU MAY REMEMBER HIS WARNINGS...
FOR THOSE OF YOU WHO DID NOT HAVE THE OPPORTUNITY TO WITTNESS DR. LEIGHTONS PREDICTIONS, HERE IS AN EXCLUSIVE EARLIER RECORDING OF MY INTERVIEW WITH DR. LEIGHTON...
"YOU WILL ALL DIE!!"
YES, THAT WAS DR. LEIGHTON 8 MONTHS AGO IN HIS DISTILLED CONNECTICUT HOME...
TO SUMMARIZE: DR. LEIGHTON PROGNOSTICATED THAT ALL FORMS OF PAIN RELIEVERS, SUCH AS THE ASPRINS THAT MANY OF US ARE ACCUSTOM TO, WILL WEAR OFF AT PRECISELY 10:31 TONIGHT.
ACCORDING TO LEIGHTON, THE HUMAN BODY NEEDS TO SUBDUE PAIN NATURALLY, AND WHEN AN ARTIFICIAL PAIN RELIEVER IS INTRODUCED, THE PAIN IS ACTUALLY STORED.
LEIGHTON HAS RECENTLY ADDED ALLERGY MEDICINES, LAXATIVES, ANTACIDS, AND SURGICAL ANESTHETICS TO HIS LIST.
WHY DO THEY MAKE THIS HARD?
LAST THING I NEED WHEN I HAVE A HEADACHE IS TO SCREW AROUND WITH THE CAP...
METAL MAYHEM '87
YOU'VE NEVER TAKEN A PAIN RELIEVER IN YOUR LIFE.
UH-HUH...
I NEED THESE THINGS...

THAT'S BETTER..
WELL, LINDA THAT WAS QUITE A PREDICTION DR. LEIGHTON MADE...AND WHERE IS HE TONIGHT, ON THE EVE OF HIS PREDICTION?
METAL
A LOT BETTER...
WELL, BRETT... AS WE ALL KNOW... DR. LEIGHTON SUFFERED FROM CHRONIC INDIGESTION... THE DISCOMFORT DROVE HIM CRAZY. REFUSING TO TAKE ANYTHING FOR IT, HIS FAMILY COMMITTED HIM...
...AND IT LOOKS AS IF WE ARE APPROACHING DR. LEIGHTON'S PREDICTION TIME.
THAT'S RIGHT, BRETT... WITH ONLY A FEW SECONDS REMAINING, LET ME TAKE A MOMENT TO TELL OUR VIEWERS ABOUT...
Eyargh!
OH MY GOD!
LADIES AND GENTLEMEN! LINDA HAS JUST FALLEN TO THE FLOOR IN A FIT OF AGONY...
ALMOST EVERYONE HERE IS SUDDENLY SCREAMING BLOODY HELL...
YES... I HAVE A CONFIRMATION... IT IS AT LEAST CITY WIDE!
DAMN...
I REPEAT! DR. LEIGHTON WAS CORRECT! WE, WHO HAVE NEVER TAKEN A PAIN RELIEVER, CAN COUNT OURSELVES LUCKY...
AARRRGH!!!
ALL THIS NOISE HAS GIVEN ME A HEADACHE!
FIRST ONE... OUCH!
OH..
SOMEONE DROPPED SOME ASPRIN.
ASPRIN
ONE... TWO... THREE...
FIN

EGG CRASH PANEL 11
?
EGG CRASH, PANEL 11?!
THAT'S NOT A TITLE!
© KPC '01
HMMM..
PERHAPS THE AUTHOR INTENDED AN ANALOGY...
A SUGGESTIVE TITLE TO HINT AT SOME UNDERSCORING EVENT THAT WILL TRANSPIRE...
SON OF A BITCH!
THIS PISSES ME OFF! SOME MAY CALL ME AN EGG! AND I CAN'T FIGURE OUT WHAT THIS IDIOT IS GETTING AT!
MAYBE HE'S RECALLING KAFKA, WITH SURREAL ENVIORNMENTS THAT TEAR AT THE VERY FABRIC OF COMPLACENCY. OR...
WAIT! THIS IS A WINDOW? NO... A DOOR? NO... IT'S A COMIC PANEL!
NOW I SEE THE WIT... AND I SEE WITH CLARITY. HIS ATTEMPT TO FOOL ME WAS A FUTILE ONE. I AM IN PANEL 7... AND THIS I SEE IS 8.
SO THAT NOW LEAVES THREE MORE PANELS UNTIL 11... WHAT HAPPENS THEN IN MY NEAR FUTURE?
AND HOW MANY WORDS CAN I RAMMBLE OFF TO POSTPONE THE INEVITABLE?
!!
CRASH
FIN

AUTUMN IN NEW ENGLAND.. THERE'S NOTHING LIKE IT...
CALM. CRISP. SERENE.
BUT, FOR A CERTAIN YOUNG MAN WITH A POOR DIET, IT WOULD PROVE COSTLY...
Kee-RYST do I have to take a DUMP!!
OH GAWD NO!! NOT
ANOTHER BAD POO STORY
BY KEITH KNIGHT
©K.KNIGHT 2001
IT ALL BEGAN WHEN MY PARENTS DROPPED ME OFF AT MY AUNT'S HOUSE FOR THE AFTERNOON..
I ALWAYS DREADED GOIN' OVER TO MY AUNT'S HOUSE CUZ SHE CALLED ME "FOOL" A LOT...
Hey, fool.
Hey, Aunt Mary.
keeflix@hotmail.com
SHE WAS A HAIRDRESSER...& SHE ALWAYS LOOKED FORWARD TO TEARING THROUGH MY NAPPY-ASS HEAD WITH HER BIG BLACK COMB OF DEATH..
Hold Still, Fool.
OW!!
BUT I WAS PREPARED THIS TIME.. I BROUGHT SOME $$$ WITH ME FOR LUNCH SO I COULD ESCAPE...
Aunt Mary!! Can I go over to Burger Queen for lunch?
Sure, fool.
YES!!
BOY WAS I PSYCHED!! IT WAS A BIT OF A WALK, BUT IT WOULD BE WORTH IT....
PLUS I KNEW THIS SHORTCUT THROUGH A HOLE IN THIS FENCE THAT WOULD CUT 20 MINUTES OFF THE TRIP...

THE SHORTCUT WENT THROUGH THE BACKYARDS OF SOME REALLY EXPENSIVE HOUSES...
THERE WAS A HUGE CONCENTRATION OF OAK & MAPLE TREES BACK THERE.. BEAUTIFUL.
IT WAS LIKE A LITTLE MINI-FOREST IN THE CITY..
EVENTUALLY, I MADE IT TO THE BURGER QUEEN & DONE THE DIRTY DEED..
URF
..AND BEGAN THE WALK BACK TO MY AUNT'S HOUSE..
♫
PUT LITTER IN ITS PLACE
NOW, I MAY HAVE THE DIET OF YOUR AVERAGE PRE-TEENAGE AFRICAN AMERICAN BOY--
ZZZZZ
ZZZZ
--BUT I HAVE THE STOMACH & BOWELS OF A 97 YEAR OLD WHITE MAN.
RUMBLE
ZZZ SNORT HUH?
RUMBLE RUMBLE
Wha--?
RUMBLE
!
INCOMING!!
SPLORK!!!

JiMiNY FRiCKiN' CRICKETS!! He's BEEN EATIN' THAT DAMNED FAST-FOOD SHITE AGAIN!!
How ARe WE SUPPOSED TO WORK WITH THIS?!! THERE'S NOTHING GOOD IN HERE!!
Why couldn't we be workin' with some sorta Hippie Vegetarian Bohemian kid or something?
Well.. SCREW IT!! We're pushin' This STUFF RIGHT OUT THE BACK DOOR.
And I'm gonna throw This box of Thumb Tacks in for good measure...
This oughta Teach Him a lesson he won't soon forget!!
ACME
Okay.. Now help me PUSH This stuff outta here.. Ready? 1-2-3-PUSH!!
OW!!..
IT WAS WEIRD. I HAD NEVER FELT SUCH SHARP PAINS IN MY ASS BEFORE..
I BEGAN TO INCREASE MY PACE..
PUSH HARDER, DAMMIT!! WE'VE GOT TO GET THIS OUT, NOW!!
OW!!..

RIGHT THEN & THERE I KNEW I WAS GONNA POO IN APPROXIMATELY 1 MINUTE..
60...59...58...57...56...55...54
& I WAS LOCATED PRECARIOUSLY BETWEEN THE BURGER QUEEN & MY AUNT'S HOUSE...
AUNTS
33..32..!?!!..31..30..29
THERE WAS NO WAY I WAS GONNA MAKE IT TO EITHER LOCATION IN TIME...
I WAS GONNA HAFTA POO IN PUBLIC.. AND THERE WAS ONLY ONE PLACE TO DO IT:
..15..14..13..12..11...10..9..
THE MINI-FOREST.
I BOOKED IT TO THE MINI-FOREST & I BARELY GOT MY PANTS DOWN FAST ENOUGH...
DUMP
Jeeeezus wept...
..3...2..1
LORD, WAS IT PAINFUL.. I TURNED TO SPY THE POO TO SEE IF THERE WERE ANY TACKS IN IT CUZ IT SURE FELT LIKE IT..
YOUR POO ALWAYS LOOKS DIFFERENT WHEN YOU SEE IT ON THE GROUND AS OPPOSED TO IN A TOILET.
*
WITH NUTZ!!
*editor may have substituted poo drawing for something easier on the eyes.
WELL.. NOW IT WAS TIME TO WIPE MY ASS.. AND THERE WERE PLENTY OF LEAVES AROUND, BUT..
crackle crinkle
..IT WAS FALL!! & THE LEAVES WERE DEAD, DRY & CRUMBLING IN MY BUTT..
NOOOOOC
HEY!!! WHO'S OUT THERE?!! GET HIM, BOY..
ROWF ROWF
!
IN RETROSPECT, I SHOULD'VE JUST WIPED WITH MY UNDIES & TOSSED THEM AWAY..
Zing

THE ARTIST WAS ACTUALLY 19 WHEN THIS HAPPENED......

IT WASN'T LIKE SHE KNEW HE WAS GOING TO DIE, HE ONLY RECENTLY TURNED 40. WHO COULD HAVE EVEN GUESSED THAT ON NEW YEARS DAY HE WOULD SIMPLY DROP DEAD? ONE MOMENT ALIVE, THE NEXT MOMENT A HEART ATTACK CLAIMING HIS LIFE.
HE FELL TO THE FLOOR AS SHE WATCHED FROM ACROSS THE ROOM. SHE RAN TO HIM IN SLOW MOTION, THE SECOND SHE LOOKED INTO HIS EYES SHE KNEW HE WAS ALREADY GONE.
THE AMBULANCE CAME AND THE PARAMEDICS TRIED TO REVIVE HIM, THEY SPED AWAY WITH HIS LIFELESS BODY.
HE WAS BURIED WHERE HE GREW UP, IN THE MIDWEST. SHE HAD TO BORROW MONEY TO PAY FOR AN AIRPLANE TICKET TO GET TO HIS FUNERAL.

BACK IN THE HOUSE THAT HAD ONCE BEEN THE HOME THEY SHARED, SHE KNEW NOT WHAT TO DO. DESPAIR HAD OVERTAKEN HER. SHE SAT IN WHAT WAS HIS FAVORITE CHAIR AND DID NOT MOVE FOR HOURS. FOR WEEKS ON END. THIS IS ALL SHE COULD DO.
ONE DAY AFTER NIGHT HAD FALLEN, SITTING IN THE DARKNESS, THE DOG BEGAN TO JUMP AROUND AND ACT ALL EXCITED, AS IF TO GREET SOMEONE. SHE WENT TO THE FRONT DOOR TO CHECK BUT ALAS, NO ONE WAS THERE. SHE THEN TURNED AROUND TO WALK BACK TO THE CHAIR. IT STARTLED HER TO SEE THE ROOM WAS NOW BATHED IN LIGHT.
THIS WAS NOT TO BE AN ISOLATED INCIDENT. OVER THE COURSE OF THE NEXT FEW MONTHS IT ACTUALLY BECAME QUITE A COMMONPLACE EVENT. SHE LIKED TO THINK IT WAS HIM, SILENTLY HELPING HER THROUGH. THIS THOUGHT, MOST LIKELY, WAS THE ONLY THING SHE HAD THAT CONVINCED HER TO GO ON.
SLOWLY HER DESPAIR BEGAN TO LOOSEN ITS DEEP GRIP EVER SO SLIGHTLY, AS DESPAIR IS APT TO DO WITH THE PASSING OF TIME. WHEN NEXT THE LIGHT TURNED ON BY ITSELF AND THE DOG RAN ABOUT SHE REALIZED THE MOMENT HAD ARRIVED TO LET GO OF HIM. SHE WAS ABLE TO SAY GOODBYE.

ROOTBEER!
by JAMES KOCHALKA
Hello, Rootbeer!
NO PARKIN
Are you a good boy?
I know, I know, you want to go for a ride. Let me unlock you.

I know you get a little lonely waiting for me.
I'm sorry.
Well, if you could remember the combination, you could unlock yourself and go for a spin whenever you wanted.
No,
I couldn't just leave you unlocked.
You'd get stolen.

huff huff
This is good exercise, huh Rootbeer?

KINKO'S
here we are
I just have to lock you up again while I make some photocopies.
the end.

the Polite Couple
WOULD YOU LIKE SOMETHING TO DRINK?
NO THANKS, I'M FINE.
SHANNON WHEELER ©2001
THIS MOVIE IS REALLY GOOD EVEN THOUGH IT'S ONLY ON TV.
I REALLY LIKE IT TOO.
I'M SORRY. AM I TALKING TOO MUCH?
NO, NO. I DON'T MIND TALKING DURING MOVIES. UNLESS IT'S A SCENE WHEN YOU DON'T WANT ME TO TALK.
YOU CAN TALK AS MUCH AS YOU LIKE. I JUST DON'T WANT TO BOTHER YOU WITH MY TALKING.
IT DOESN'T BOTHER ME.
GREAT. THEN WE CAN TALK AS MUCH AS WE LIKE.
IT'S GOOD THAT WE BOTH LIKE TO TALK.

THE DIRECTOR OF THIS MOVIE IS REALLY GOOD.
YOU THINK SO?
MAYBE NOT. I USED TO LIKE HIM. BUT NOW, I DON'T KNOW. HIS NEW STUFF ISN'T AS GOOD.
I USED TO LIKE HIM TOO.
I DIDN'T SEE HIS SECOND MOVIE BECAUSE IT GOT BAD REVIEWS.
I DON'T BELIEVE IN REVIEWS.
WHY NOT?
CRITICS SEE MOVIES ALL DAY LONG. THEIR TASTES ARE WARPED BY OVEREXPOSURE TO MOVIES.
I HATE HOW THEY SPOIL PLOTS. IF THEY'D JUST GIVE ME THEIR OPINION WITHOUT RUINING THE SUPRISE OF THE FILM I WOULD LIKE THEM BETTER.
I LIKE GOOD MOVIES.
ME TOO.

FINALLY, A COMMERCIAL.
DO YOU LIKE COMMERCIALS?
NO. I HATE THEM. I DIDN'T WANT TO SAY ANYTHING, BUT I'VE HAD TO GO TO THE BATHROOM FOR THE LAST HALF HOUR.
HALF HOUR?
I DIDN'T WANT TO BOTHER YOU BY GETTING UP.
THAT'S FUNNY.
FUNNY?
I'VE HAD TO GO TOO, BUT I DIDN'T WANT TO BOTHER YOU.
IF YOU HAVE TO GO, YOU SHOULD GO ON AHEAD AND I'LL WAIT.
PLEASE. YOU GO. YOU'VE BEEN WAITING.
I MIGHT BE A WHILE. YOU GO FIRST.
I HATE THE IDEA OF YOU WAITING WHILE I'M GOING. YOU SHOULD GO.
OOPS. IT LOOKS LIKE THE SHOW HAS STARTED AGAIN.

HOW'S IT GOIN'?

THAT'S REALLY INTERESTING
GOOD LUCK WITH THAT!
I'LL SEE YA LATER
BYE!

WHY IS MY DENTIST SO WEIRD?
BY PETER S. CONRAD
WHY DO DENTISTS ALWAYS HAVE THICK BUSHY HAIR AND EYEBROWS? AND BIG PORES?
MY FRIEND JOE SAYS:
DUDE... I TRIED THAT DENTIST YOU RECOMMENDED.
HE'S A LITTLE *ROUGH*.
HIS OFFICE IS DOWNTOWN.
FIRE
IT'S KIND OF DINGY...
...AND GRIMY.
I'M PRETTY SURE HE CLEANS ALL HIS INSTRUMENTS BETWEEN CLIENTS.
805
HOWARD M. ELBOWSTEIN D.D.S.
8 FLOOR
1

I WENT IN LAST WEEK FOR A CLEANING.
I HAD A CAVITY.
UH-OH... LOOK WHAT I FOUND!
WANT ME TO TAKE CARE OF THAT RIGHT NOW?
SHUHR.
SO... DO YOU REALLY WANT ANESTHETIC? IT'S ONLY THREE SECONDS OF DRILLING... AND IT'LL ONLY HURT FOR TWO OF THE SECONDS.
UH...
SOME PEOPLE DON'T WANT ANESTHETIC.
HOW MUCH WILL IT HURT?
YOU KNOW-- FORGET IT! I'D BETTER NUMB YOU UP...
I MEAN... IF YOU HAVE TO THINK ABOUT IT.
2

CRANK CRANK CRANK
N--NNGH!
CRANK CRANK CRANK
I KNOW IT HURTS.
I HAVE TO BE SURE I HIT THE *NERVE TRUNK*.
CRANK CRANK
PEOPLE'S NERVES AREN'T ALWAYS IN THE SAME PLACE.
PEOPLE'S NERVES AREN'T IN THE SAME PLACE?
NOTE TO SELF: KEEP EYES CLOSED. NOTHING LIKE GETTING A CHIP OF YOUR OWN TOOTH IN YOUR EYE.
BZZZZZZZ
HOT TEETH SMELL BAD.
3

I'VE HAD OTHER WEIRD DENTISTS...
BEFORE AIDS WE DIDN'T WEAR GLOVES. IT WAS JUST GLORIOUS BLOOD EVERYWHERE
ALL I DO IS TAKE TEETH OUT. IT'S WHAT I LIKE TO DO.
BUT THIS GUY TAKES THE CAKE.
...HAND ME THE LARGE COMPRESSOR.
YOU WANT ME TO FILE YOUR FRONT TEETH DOWN A BIT?
NO THANKS.
THERE'S NO CHARGE...
NO THANKS.
SUIT YOURSELF.
UH...DO THE CAVITRON, GET A COUPLE OF BITEWINGS AND ANTERIORS...
YES, DOCTOR.
HIS STAFF IS KIND OF WEIRD, TOO.
ISN'T THAT GOING TO X-RAY MY BRAIN?
DON'T BE SILLY!
4
END.

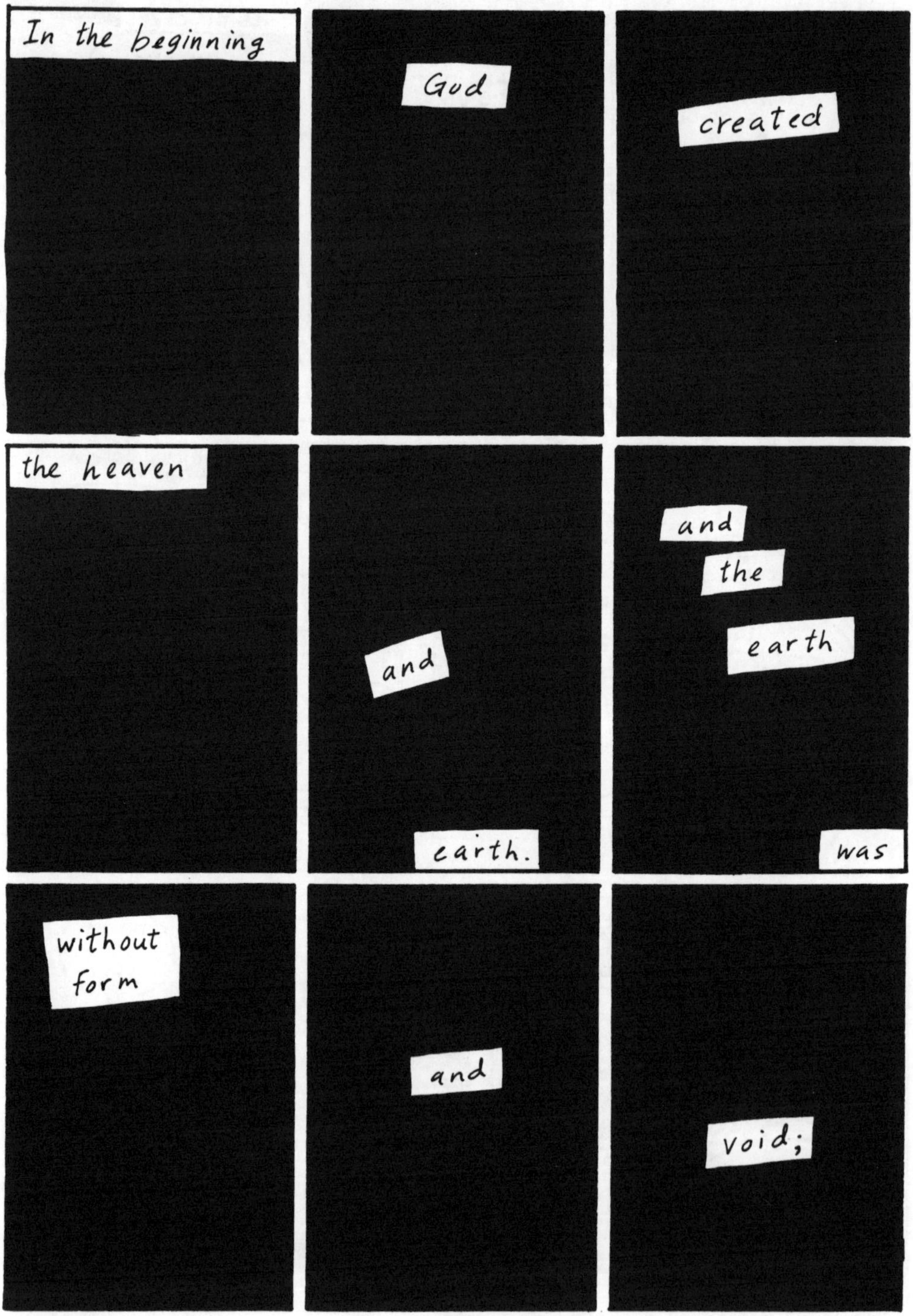
In the beginning
God
created
the heaven
and
earth.
and
the
earth
was
without
form
and
void;

and
darkness
was
upon
the face
of the deep.
And the spirit of God
moved upon
the
face
of
the waters.
and God said,
Let there be light:

TEXT: Old Testament, King James Version, ca. 1611, ART: David Lasky, June 2001

SOLACE
This doesn't belong here.

One morning, when I was very young, I woke up early and fixed myself some breakfast.
Nobody else was awake.
This must have been a Saturday; otherwise, my father would have been up.
I smelled cat food.
And so it must have been summer. The heat always brought out the smell of cat food in the kitchen.
Suddenly, my grandfather was there, sitting across from me.

I don't remember him coming into the kitchen.
Maybe he was there when I came in.
Perhaps I didn't notice him at first.

It takes a while for my eyes to adjust to a new room.
I couldn't look at him.

Once in a while, as a sort of escape, he'd take a commuter train to Chicago and watch the Cubs.
He kept score meticulously.
Before the game, he might buy a new pen.
He parceled out solace for himself.
That may not be accurate. I write, "He parceled out solace for himself" because it seems to be true of me.
I looked away from him, down at the cat food.
Sometimes you enter a room and someone's there.

Your hat's inside.
I'll be right out.
Turn off the patio light.
Okay.
Do I want a grandson who cannot look at me?
I do.
J. HANKIEWICZ '01

HELP ME, MAMA.
Donna Barr ©01
OR... I'm going to bury my telephone...
RING!
Hallo?
Oh, hi, Emma. Cat's are fine. Huh? No, I haven't seen where the new neighbors have put their dog-pen. Why?
Uh-huh. Well, have Al tell 'em to move the pen, if it's too near your fence. Huh? The guy over here— well, I couldn't tell you if he's gay or not. We just live by him. Huh?
1/2-hour later...
Yes, they're very nice people. No, I don't know if she's pregnant. No, I don't know if they're married...
I don't know why she calls... I don't know any gossip!
She's 92— I gotta be polite.
Whew!
!
RING!
Hallo? Oh, hi, Josef. Huh? I thought you were getting along with your new girlfriend.
What?

Oh~ with your girlfriend's boyfriend? Huh?
Well, if he IS bullying you, how is that HER problem? Just tell him to back off...
They're adults— let 'em take care of themselves.
Look~ you're calling from Germany~ isn't this EXPENSIVE?
If her friend doesn't speak English, how are you humiliating her? Does she HAVE to speak English?
Oh... you— have really good rates.
Oh, JOY.
RING RING RING
What? NO, Roberta,* I will NOT get up early tomorrow to go down to City hall and help you file for bankruptcy!
RING RING RING RING
* Not Roberta Gregory
Oh, Crap— Ellaine's drunk and CHATTY again.
Ellaine, I'm very happy you've come out as a lesbian ~ but if you want to go to Seattle to hang out at the Wild Rose bar, I can't help you— I don't know anybody there. Go yourself— lesbians don't BITE.
RING
DONNA! HELP! There's a man looking in at my window! Call the police! I'm SCARED!
DIAL 911, Idiot! Am I the only one with a PHONE!?
Nooo... GO AWAY!
Oh, I HATE the answering machine! I'm calling from Ireland and just HAVE to chat!
RING RING RING
I have to get your advice about this ROCK I bought!

new shoes
SPLUTCH!
the end.

noodles and nativity.
MO-O-OMMA? WAS I BORN OUT OF A ROCK LIKE SUN WUKONG THE MONKEY KING?
OR MA-A-AYBE OUT OF A LOTUS FLOWER HATCHED FROM AN EGG LIKE NEZHA WHO FOUGHT WITH THE DRAGON KING?
OR, OR, OR WAS I BORN OUT OF A PEACH LIKE MOMOTARO IN POPPA'S STORY FROM NIHON?
NO, MY PLUM, YOU WERE BORN OUT OF MOMMA'S BELLY.
the end.

ANGIE'S WORLD
"DETENTION"
©2001 FC BRANDT
MISTER CAMEO, HOW MUCH LONGER DO I HAVE TO **SIT QUIET** FOR?
BUT I *DIDN'T* TALK FIRST! I WAS JUST ANSWERING PETEY'S QUESTION HE ASKED ME, AND **THEN** --
OKAY.
ATH
GOOD JOB
THIS
THAT
WHERE ARE YOU GOING?
YES, I'LL BE **GOOD** WHILE YOU'RE GONE, BUT...
...CAN I **DRAW**?

OH! I COULD HAVE? OKAY. THANKS!
GEE, I COULDA BEEN DRAWING THIS WHOLE TIME! I THOUGHT I HAD TO JUST SIT ALL QUIET.
HM... WHICH TO USE?
HEY, ANGIE! LOOKIT WHAT I FOUND!!
EEW!! GROSS, TONY!
HELLO, ANGIE. I'VE BEEN SENT TO GIVE TO YOU THIS MAGICAL PEN.
SUPER!

OH, WAIT!
WHAT WAS THAT OTHER STUFF SHE SAID?
...MAGICAL PEN. IT IS A GIFT OF WONDEROUS POWERS, AND IT IS GRANTED TO YOU BY THE QUEEN OF PATRONIA.
BUT TAKE CARE, YOUNG ANGIE. THIS PEN IS NOT A TOY, IT IS A TOOL CAPABLE OF THINGS GREAT AND...
...AND...
...AND...
...AND...
...AND...
...AAAAND...

SOMETHING SOMETHING SOMETHING SO
SOMETHING SOMETHING SOMETHING SOMETHI
SOMETHING SOMETHING SOMETHING SOMETHING
HM... I THINK I'LL DRAW A LION!
HA! TONY CAN'T WHISTLE.
...if I only had a heart...
TCH! I HATE DRAWING HANDS.
...AND LAST, A TAIL...
...DONE!
RAWR!!!

ROWR! GRRR! GROWR
HEY!! WHA?
OH, MY!
LOOK AT YOU. WHAT A HANDSOME LION YOU ARE.
CAN YOU TALK?
NO? WELL, ARE YOU A GOOD LION? YOU'RE A GOOD BOY, AREN'T YOU?
eep!
ZIP

HEY!
GRRRRR GRRR GRR
LEAP!
CUT THAT OUT! GET DOWN FROM THERE.
OH! STOP! WHAT A BAD LION YOU ARE!!
RRRRRRRRRRR
RIP! TEAR! REND!
SCRATCH! SCRATCH! SCRAPE!
NO! DON'T BREAK THE WINDOW.
THUMP!
BAD LION! STAY!! DON'T YOU GO OUT THERE.
SKREEEK
OH, NO.
'BYE.

The Year of LOVING DANGEROUSLY
BY TED RALL
IT WAS ALL KAREN'S FAULT. AFTER ALL, SHE WAS THE ONE WHO SPENT TENNIS CAMP DOING A DOUBLES CHAMP FROM FORT WAYNE, INDIANA IN THE SHOWER.
YO! TED'S ON THE PHONE FROM NEW YORK!
LATER!
ACTUALLY, IT WAS BARBARA'S FAULT FOR TELLING ME ALL THE GORY DETAILS. BARBARA WAS KAREN'S BEST FRIEND IN THE WHOLE WORLD.
SHE SAID HE WAS HUGE! THAT IT WAS THE BEST LAY SHE'D EVER—
STOP! I CAN'T STAND TO HEAR ANOTHER WORD! WELL? WHAT ELSE?
THE OUTCOME OF BARBARA'S REVELATION WAS INEVITABLE.
STRANGE... I DON'T FEEL ANY GUILT AT ALL!
I'VE ALWAYS LOVED YOU!
I RAN INTO KAREN A FEW DAYS LATER...
YOU SCREWED MY BEST FRIEND?!
WAIT! NOW WE'RE SQUARE! NOW WE CAN MOVE ON... TOGETHER!

IT DIDN'T TAKE LONG FOR EVERY WOMAN IN MANHATTAN TO FIND OUT I WAS SINGLE. I DECIDED TO AVAIL MYSELF OF EVERY OPPORTUNITY.
YO YOURSELF. DUMPED, HUH?
YO.
I WAS HAVING THE TIME OF MY LIFE, YET SOMETHING WAS MISSING.
HEY, THIS IS JUST LIKE "RISKY BUSINESS"!
EACH WOMAN I HAD SEX WITH PUT KAREN FURTHER FROM MY THOUGHTS. EACH ONE MADE ME FEEL MORE CONFIDENT. BETTER. MORE NUMB.
YOUR HUSBAND DOESN'T LOVE YOU. I CAN TELL.
THE SUMMER WAS IMPOSSIBLY HOT. EVERYONE'S MINDS WERE AS DIRTY AS THE NEW YORK AIR, AND I NEEDED IT EVERY NIGHT FROM SOMEONE NEW.
IT'S NICOLE.
TELL HER I DIED. SPIDERS OR SOMETHING.
I DID OKAY ON MY OWN, BUT I KNEW I COULD DO BETTER WITH A PARTNER IN CRIME, SINCE GIRLS OFTEN TRAVEL BARS IN PAIRS.
YER ON!
2

JIM WAS A HORNY GUY'S DREAM PARTNER. HE SUFFERED FROM A FETISH THAT ENSURED THAT WE NEVER, EVER FOUGHT OVER WHO PAIRED UP WITH WHOM.
DIBS ON THE UGLY ONE! SHE'LL BE GRRREAT!
KILL MEN
BECAUSE JIM ONLY LIKED TOTAL HEIFERS, I ALWAYS GOT THE PICK OF AVAILABLE WOMEN.
I FEEL SORRY FOR YOUR FRIEND.
DON'T! YOU'D MAKE HIM WANNA BLOW CHUNKS!
JIM AND I WENT OUT SCAMMING FOR GIRLS EVERY NIGHT. AND, THANKS TO HIS LOW STANDARDS, WE WERE USUALLY SUCCESSFUL.
BATHING IS A CULTURAL CONSTRUCT! IF YOU ASK ME, IT'S TOTALLY OVERRATED.
R.E.M. WOULDN'T EXIST IF NOT FOR WIRE!
EVENTUALLY, I GOT SO GOOD AT MEETING AND PICKING UP WOMEN THAT I COULD GO TO A GIRL'S HOUSE, HAVE SEX, AND RETURN TO THE SAME BAR TO PICK UP A SECOND ONE.
YOU WERE HERE BEFORE, RIGHT?
UM, NO.
3
THEN I GOT FIRED.
WALL ST.

I DIDN'T REALLY CARE THAT I'D BEEN FIRED (FOR STEALING SOMETHING I HADN'T TAKEN) SINCE IT WAS A CRUMMY JOB ANYWAY. STILL, I'D BEEN LIVING HAND-TO-MOUTH AND, A MONTH LATER, I WAS SHIT OUT OF LUCK.
6C
City of New York
EVICTION
I SPENT A NIGHT RIDING BACK AND FORTH ON THE 7TH AVENUE LOCAL, RIDING IN AIR-CONDITIONED, IMPOVERISHED COMFORT.
MY FLIRTATION WITH HOMELESSNESS ENDED WHEN I DECIDED TO USE WHAT I KNEW BEST—SEX—TO GET BACK ON MY FEET. I WOULDN'T LET MYSELF GO. I WOULD NEVER SLEEP ON A SUBWAY TRAIN AGAIN!
2 BR SUBLET FEMALE ONLY 864-1702
Rental WOMEN ONLY 212 W.96
share 1 BR w/pervert
THAT NIGHT, I HIT THE CATHEDRAL CAFE, THE WEST END AND THE MARLIN WITH ONE MISSION IN MIND: FIND A FEMALE HUMAN BEING WHO'D LET ME CRASH UNTIL I COULD LAND A JOB AND AN APARTMENT.
HEY.
HEY.
4

IT WAS A SIMPLE TRADE-OFF: AN ORGASM OR TWO FOR A NIGHT OF SLEEP UNDER LAURA ASHLEY SHEETS AND ACCESS TO A FULLY-EQUIPPED BATHROOM.
I'M OFF TO WORK. YOU CAN LET YOURSELF OUT.
TWO WEEKS WENT BY LIKE THAT. FOURTEEN BARS ON THE UPPER WEST SIDE. FOURTEEN ONE-NIGHT STANDS. FOURTEEN SHORT-TERM SUBLETS.
THANK GOD FOR THAT INTERVIEW TOMORROW!
FINALLY I FOUND A JOB MATCHING FILE FOLDERS WITH STRAY DOCUMENTS. I USED THE NEW JOB TO RENT A SMALL ONE-BEDROOM ON WEST 102ND STREET.
AND HERE'S THE KEY!
SUCKER!
I THREW A PARTY TO CELEBRATE. NATURALLY, I INVITED JIM. NATURALLY, WE SCORED A PAIR OF FRATERNAL TWINS FROM LONG ISLAND BEFORE THE COPS ARRIVED.
YOU HAVE THE MOST PERFECT CHEST IN THE WHOLE WORLD!
THAT FALL, ONE WOMAN AFTER ANOTHER PASSED THROUGH MY LIFE. BY LATE DECEMBER I WAS DATING AN 18-YEAR-OLD HIGH SCHOOL JUNIOR FROM THE BRONX.
CAN I INVITE MY FRIENDS TO YOUR NEW YEAR'S PARTY?
SURE!
5
ON NEW YEAR'S EVE MY FRIEND CHRIS FED ME HASH BROWNIES AND RUM-AND-COKES. I THINK I REMEMBER HAVING EATEN EIGHT BROWNIES.
THESE THINGS DON'T WORK! GIMME MORE!

I WOKE UP THE NEXT DAY, BUT IT WAS ALREADY NIGHT. JIM WAS KNOCKING ON MY DOOR ABOUT A HUGE WOMAN HE'D DONE. I WAS IN BED WITH MY GIRLFRIEND AND HER LITTLE SISTER.
TED! I NEED A MORNING-AFTER PILL!
THEY WERE NUMBERS 45 AND 46 OF THAT YEAR'S GIRLS.
I DECIDED THEN AND THERE TO REFORM. NO MORE PROMISCUITY. NO MORE HASH BROWNIES. NO MORE SEX AS A MEANS OF FINDING HOUSING.
I LOST TRACK OF JIM. MY LIFE BECAME MORE SEDATE. I GOT A STEADY GIRLFRIEND, A REAL JOB AND STARTED TO PAY OFF DEBTS.
SURE YOU DON'T WANNA GO OUT?
ABSOLUTELY.
YEARS LATER, I RAN INTO JIM AT THE MARLIN BAR.
YOU LOOK AWFUL!
OF COURSE! AIDS HAS A WAY OF DOING THAT.
I DIDN'T GO TO KANSAS FOR THE FUNERAL. WHAT WOULD HAVE BEEN THE POINT?
JIM AND I LIVED THE SAME LIFE. THERE'S NO MORAL: I WON; HE LOST. SOMETIMES I MISS JIM. SOMETIMES I MISS THAT YEAR.
LOOK AT THAT COW - SHE'LL BE GRRREAT!
TR
6